THE MARINER

ERIC DEAN CAMPBELL

DEDICATION

To those who are unable to escape the violence of mankind.

Eric Dean Campbell

CONTENTS

Eric Dean Campbell

ILLUSTRATIONS

Eric Dean Campbell

ACKNOWLEDGMENTS

Bert Parkin and Keith Maurer were brilliant, humble men
who lived in a different age. They believed children
deserved to be taught art, literature, scripture and what it
means to be a global citizen on this planet. They believed
all men and women were equal, all had a contribution to
make; all deserving of respect.

Though they have long since passed, I can proudly say
their teachings abound in my thoughts daily.

Eric Dean Campbell

Greifswald Harbor
Greifwalder Hafen c.1819
Caspar David Friedrich
Alte Nationalgalerie

Eric Dean Campbell

THE MARINER

I met an old man with crippled up hands
who claimed he had worked the sea.
He pulled out his knife and said
"This be my strife I tells to all strangers, now ye".

I stopped of a sudden, this man was curmudgeon
and obviously I was his plan.
He made it quite clear I was going to hear
his story or bleed if I ran.

A strong man was he; violence, you see
was still well within his power.
Though I am not small, this old man was tall,
and o'er me did he tower.

"When I was in Clink, it gave time to think
and recover from horrors" he cried.
"The square meals they gave kept me from the grave
though better if I'd not survived."

Eric Dean Campbell

He spoke of a wife who was skilled with a knife
and of "children who died in the sea.
They be sons of the gun, yet I loved them"
he sung, in a haunting and soft melody.

I listened to him with expression quite grim.
'Your wife, is she here and of help?'
"No, I am alone and without a home.
No place to escape from the kelp."

Some others did gather; they had heard his chatter
for he was quite loud, yet afraid.
Praise god they were near for I was in fear.
They sensed this was no masquerade.

"A young man was I when I first lost the eye,
so sailing' I chose for my years.
A slaver and whaler" spat the old sailor.
"I be differin' from you cavaliers."

He spoke to us four his troublesome lore
and horrors while sailing the sea.
"Listen you will, you men of the krill,
it be I, it be you and these three.

Through storm swell or calm the 'Lady' sailed on.
No finer ship for profiteer.
Come hell or high tide our ship was our pride.
My capt'n was no brigadier.

Twas back in fourteen when the captain did dream
of the riches from Hispaniola.
We'd hunted for whale 'til he put forth his sail
and landed in curs'ed Tortuga.

THE MARINER

When best years had passed and the 'Lady' would last
I'm bettin' four seasons or three,
my capt'n went knave; 'The ship's near the grave
but there's profit in slaving with me.'

Eric Dean Campbell

The Stages of Life
Die Lebensstufen c. 1835
Caspar David Friedrich
Museum der bildenden Künste

Beach in fog c. 1807
Caspar David Friedrich
Österreichische Galerie Belvedere

Eric Dean Campbell

Two men contemplating the moon c.1825
Caspar David Friedrich
Metropolitan Museum of Art

THE MARINER

A' fore Desalin the islands did seem
a haven for sailors of Gael.
Though slaves did we buy twas one caught my eye,
a younglin' who were not for sale.

The first mate he knew from which well that she drew
her water for master and home.
We waited in dark, with lust in our heart
and long knives if she took to moan.

Bos'n held her still 'til we each had our fill.
'Ye must put her down when we're done'.
'Don't worry' says I, 'the young whore'll die
but not til we all's had our fun.'

No tear did she cry. A look in her eye
had stayed me from slittin' her throat.
The first mate he said 'if we don't leave her dead
we probably should pay her the groat.'

Again she was passed; twas me to go last.
Once finished she started to quail.
I peered through the dark, til seeing our barque.
The Lady was ready to sail.

I heard to my mind, a sound from behind.
The men thought I be afraid.
'Away with your fear, I hears them draw'r near;
I'm thinkin' we're getting' waylaid.'

Her master had come. My shipmates did run,
for he carried whip and the sword.
'Unhand her' he said, 'til I stabbed him dead,
and dragged my pretty cargo aboard.

Eric Dean Campbell

Chalk Cliffs on Rügen
Kreidefelsen auf Rügen c.1825
Caspar David Friedrich
Museum Oskar Reinhart am Stadtgarte

THE MARINER

My capt'n spoke true: 'Ye share her with crew.
House her in the fo'c'sle' said he.
'When not being used or beaten and bruised,
your woman be workin' for me.'

That woman I stole was blacker than coal
and had no use to us, but fun.
Ours, body and soul, her spirit's dark toll
twas changing my shipmates, each one.

That island vodou she practiced in view,
so shipmates they left her to me.
I'd not give her back when she stabbed through the mack,
the first mate while drinking his tea.

I found her tied down. They'd passed her 'round
then cut off her hair and a thumb.
'Let's gouge out her eyes' but to my surprise
the woman asked only for rum.

'Boys' said then I, 'the woman shan't die
for I'll wed her come next feast of Pasque.'
I saw to her pain, and girded her shame
then gave her a sip from the flask.

The sailors called out 'If she lives without doubt,
we'll kill ye for what she has wrought.'
T'was bearing my son so I beat them, each one
'til all who'd been threat'ning' I'd fought.

Twas during the fray when I'd turned away,
I'd not noticed she'd gone below.
She'd ran to the hold, in spite of the cold
and spoke with the slave Georges Biassou.

Eric Dean Campbell

Georges Biassou c.1806
Juan López Cancelada or unknown

THE MARINER

Was there she did yell 'he'll save them from hell'
so loudly twas heard on the prow.
'Away from him wench' I said through the stench,
'there's nothing he'll do for ye now.'

The night came at last. Twas without lambaste
I told her to cook us our sup.
She gave then to me Valerian tea,
the strongest that ever saw cup.

It seemed though the taste could have been poppy laced.
Afore long my senses were slow.
I slept many nights, nah' hearing the fights.
Days later I woke up below.

I crawled to the deck. The ship was a wreck.
It reeked of men's death and of myrrh.
The slaves were set free. They'd killed all but me,
for I was protected by her.

Of lives I saw ten. I asked of my men.
She told how the sailors had died.
T'was she broke the latch; swords cut like thatch,
the bodies thrown o'er the side.

'The taíno you drank kept you off the plank.
We killed, then I danced while they sang.'
The smoke from her spell was keeping them well.
'We sail now to Saint Domingue.'

She ordered the ship be beached on the strip.
The rocks broke my Lady in twain.
Scuttled she be; the slaves all set free,
twas then I did ask for her name.

Eric Dean Campbell

Wreck in the Moonlight c. 1835
Caspar David Friedrich
Alte Nationalgalerie

Meeresstrand mit Fischer c. 1807
Caspar David Friedrich
Österreichische Galerie Belvedere

Eric Dean Campbell

Abend am Fluss c. 1820
Caspar David Friedrich
Wallraf Richartz Museum

THE MARINER

'My name is the lie, Wai'tu Kubuli.
We make now a home for our sons.'
To make her my wife, she drew a bone knife
to mingle our blood, and be one.

I built us a shack near the woods of Le Cap.
Wai'tu was the village bokor.
Three sons she did bare and a daughter to spare;
all of them numbering four.

One day after fast the villagers massed.
Wai'tu yelled 'We go make a plan!'
'You all come with me, to set our folk free.
We travel to Lagon å Kayiman.'

She dressed blue and gold and led young and old
through forest to some sacred tree.
They danced a queer jig then stuck a black pig.
They drank the blood as it flowed free.

They swore there that night to kill all folk white,
and chanted in tongue strange to hear.
Wai'tu danced by fire as wood they piled higher.
The look in her eyes gave me fear.

Twas Georges Biassou there, who spoke to me square.
'This girl that you took as your whore;
a young girl you stole but possessing her soul
is Lwa, Ezili Dantor.'

At hearing that name Wai'tu left the flame
and placed her hands over my head.
She muttered a spell from what I could tell.
Jeannot Bullet wanted me dead.

Eric Dean Campbell

Waldinneres bei Mondschein c. 1823
Caspar David Friedrich
Alte Nationalgalerie

The Lonely Tree
Der einsame Baum c.1822
Caspar David Friedrich
Alte Nationalgalerie

Eric Dean Campbell

Jeannot Bullet
Toussaint l'Ouverture c.1830
Unknown

THE MARINER

They pressed all around, with weapons they found.
'Sacrifice!' chanted loud.
A man to be praised was Biassou with arms raised,
fighting to keep still the crowd.

'Masters are white. We kill one tonight!'
Jeannot Bullet did yell.
My blade had been drawn yet still he pressed on.
I swore that I'd send him to hell.

They threw mud and stones, sticks, even bones.
When Wai'tu screamed they fell as though dead.
'This man no one harms. He wears Bon Dieu charms.
This one is an ancient Lwa, Ghede.'

The fear in their eyes it gave me surprise.
Wai'tu then did call me their brother.
Her rage remained hot;
'The dead he has caught, but I am Ezili The Mother.'

We left there that night, though most fled in fright.
My woman began that uprisin'.
The slaves that she led would plan to make dead
any who they were despisin'.

I thought if she dies, they'll scatter like flies.
Perchance some white lives I could save.
Strong though I were, no man could break her.
I couldn't send her to the grave.

To rid her of me I'd set Wai'tu free
from possession by Ezili Dantor.
My children I'd drown; the shack I'd burn down.
I'd make her no longer 'The Mother'.

Eric Dean Campbell

The Abbey in the Oakwood
Abtei im Eichwald c. 1809
Caspar David Friedrich
Alte Nationalgalerie

The Monk by the Sea
Der Mönch am Meer c. 1808
Caspar David Friedrich
Alte Nationalgalerie

Eric Dean Campbell

Into the sea, I took them with me,
the whelps that I'd bred from that whore.
The sea god was fair, he knew we were there
and made them Lwa no more.

I offered my sons and daughter of one,
and watched the sea god devour.
I made them unborn, my goats without horn,
and broke Ezili Dantor's power.

Mother no more, Ezili the whore
departed the flesh of Wai'tu.
The bitch left behind was the one we did find,
the one who I stole for my crew.

Wai'tu screamed at the sun and started to run.
Before she was caught, she'd went far.
I grabbed at her arm while she raised alarm.
I yelled 'Wife to me you are!

Remember your name? From where have you came?'
I screamed, grabbing her hair.
'I not be your wife sir! I swear on my life sir!
My name is Maria St. Clare!'

The girl spoke the truth. She seemed but a youth.
Wai'tu and Ezili no more.
I now knew her not, for possessed when we caught,
the puppet of Ezili Dantor.

I left her back home, the rest is unknown.
I think that she may have survived.
I saw ships in port, and as a resort
signed on with the first that arrived.

Times of day: The evening
Tageszeitenzyklus: Der Abend
Caspar David Friedrich
Lower Saxony State Museum

Eric Dean Campbell

The wanderer above the sea of fog
Der Wanderer über dem Nebelmeer c. 1817
Caspar David Friedrich
Hamburger Kunsthalle

THE MARINER

They were a good crew, though none of them knew
why that day in haste, we departed.
When we sailed away from the islands that day,
rebellion had already started.

I bunked the men. Twas round about then
the children I'd drowned came to play.
A voice whispered low that "no man should know"
the story I've told ye today.

Twas after some time the ghosts in my mind,
those voices did fill me with fury.
I killed all the crew, for one of them
knew the reason I'd not face a jury.

I see them all now; the children, the sow,
possessed by the damned voudou queen.
She tells me to kill. She's not had her fill
of souls she did ask me to glean.

I'll no longer run. It's time this be done.
I'll finish her rule over me.
You'll write out my tale on bone of the whale
and I'll take it into the sea."

He screamed "Can ye write?" then with all his might
he pushed up my face to his eyes.
"I can" I did say. He turned then away
and said "best be not scribing lies.

No paper have I, but soft as your eye
for carving is weathered baleen."
He handed his knife, "write of my wife
and children, the tale you did glean.

Eric Dean Campbell

Sailing ship
Segelschiff c. 1815
Caspar David Friedrich
Kunstsammlungen Chemnitz

THE MARINER

My killin must end. I'm plannin' to send
my flesh to the god of the sea.
I want him to read of all of the deed
afore he takes charge over me."

He buttoned his coat, and sat as I wrote.
"You men will sit here til' I'm free.
I'll jump from the spar. Witness you are.
You and companions three."

The last words were done. I'd wrote every one.
The mariner, he looked satisfied.
"I'll send to the void this tale of mine, boy.
Tis time for this sailor to die.

Toss to the deep and none of it keep,
this tale not meant for thee."
Thus we finished the tome upon polished bone,
the mariner, I and three.

Though old now I am, I wonder if when,
the sailor sank under the waves,
were his gods offended, or was he commended
for hundreds he'd sent to their graves.

I write down this tale, the one writ on whale,
on paper for all who will read.
Enough time at last I think now has passed
to write of the tale he told me.

The last thing he cried just before the man died
still haunts me and will for my life.
"Ezili is there! Beside you, beware!"
For just then arrived my dear wife.

Eric Dean Campbell

Moonrise over the Sea
Mondaufgang am Meer c. 1822
Caspar David Friedrich
Alte Nationalgalerie

THE MARINER

It wasn't my shame at hearing the name
that left me in horror back then;
it was the words she did cry when she watched the man
die: "Agwe, I now start again."

My wife was away for most of today.
Our children I've placed to be found.
For when she returns, she will learn
that both of our children I've drowned.

End.

Eric Dean Campbell

Woman before the Rising Sun
Frau vor untergehender Sonne c.1818
Caspar David Friedrich
Museum Folkwang

Eric Dean Campbell

SYNOPSIS

Act 1

The narrator is stopped by an old sailor who threatens to kill him if he runs. He begins his horrifying tale as 3 others listen in.

Scene 1
Our narrator is on his way home when he passes the ship docks. A tall, well-muscled but old mariner threatens him with a knife if he runs away. They sit. The unnamed mariner begins telling a tale of how he first got into sailing after losing his eye. The mariner is alone in the world, having lost his wife and having had his children all drown. He relates how after years of whaling, his captain decides to go on a final mission with the aging ship named "Lady". This will be a journey to the Caribbean to purchase slaves.

Scene 2

After loading the ship with slaves, the men see a young woman who they desire to gang rape and kill. Once they have raped her, the sailor decides to keep her alive but take her on the ship to use as pleasure for the crew. Before they can make it to the "Lady" the girl's owner finds them and demands she be released. The crew runs except for the mariner, who stabs the man dead and takes the girl aboard.

Scene 3

While at sea the crew regularly mistreats and rapes the young woman, with the captain's approval. When not being used, the woman is to be servant to the captain. The woman begins practicing voudou within view of the crew, who allow her this small freedom. Unfortunately the voudou seems to be having a negative effect on the crew.

Scene 4

While drinking tea, the young woman stabs and kills the first mate. The crew bind her, cut off her hair and amputate one of her thumbs. As they are about to gouge out her eyes the mariner intervenes and states that he will marry her. As he tends to her wounds, the crew threaten to kill them both. Since she is pregnant, the mariner fights the entire crew and ends the matter.

Scene 5

During the fighting, the young woman goes to the hold of the ship where she meets up with the slave Georges Biassou (who a few short years later will lead one of history's only successful slave rebellions). When the mariner finds her speaking with Biassou, she yells out that he will save them all. The mariner replies 'not now'.

Scene 6
That night the mariner orders the woman to prepare the evening meal. She serves him drugged tea that puts him to sleep for several days. He wakes in the hold, crawls to the deck and realizes that his crew are missing and the slaves have the ship. The woman answers his questions about the battle, stating she was the one who released and armed the slaves. She then explains how she saved his life by drugging him before the battle.

Scene 7
The ship returns to the islands and is wrecked deliberately on a reef. The mariner asks the young woman her name. She goes by the false name of "Wai 'tu Kubuli". She then cuts them both mingling their blood in a marriage ceremony.

Act 2

The mariner attempts to build a life with his wife and children, but discovers his wife has a secret.

Scene 1
The mariner builds a shack in a village by a forest. Wai 'tu becomes the village "bokor" or priestess. She and the mariner are quietly raising their four children when Wai 'tu arranges for a meeting in a sacred area of the forest near Alligator Lagoon. There, the mariner again encounters George's Biassou who informs him that Wai 'tu is actually possessed by a spirit named "Ezili Dantor". Another slave by the name of Jeannot Bullet, who had also been in the ship's hold, is present as well. Bullet insists the mariner should be the first of the white masters to die in their revolt. While Biassou tries calming the crowd, they begin chanting and attacking until Wai 'tu suddenly and loudly proclaims that the mariner is actually a spirit named "Ghede". She goes on to state that "Ghede" is doing god's

work by collecting the dead. Angry, Wai 'tu finally reveals herself to all as the spirit "Ezili", the Lwa of Motherhood. Many of the participants flee at this point. Those who stay plan a slave revolt under the direction of Wai 'tu.

Scene 2

The mariner, in an attempt to stop the revolt and prevent mass killing, decides that if Wai 'tu is free of "Ezili Dantor" the revolt will not happen. As "Ezili" is "The Mother", the mariner realizes if he drowns their children, she will no longer be able to possess Wai 'tu. As he leads the children into the sea, the mariner asks the sea god to take them in death, removing any spirits that may be possessing them as well. Once they have died, Ezili leaves the flesh of Wai 'tu.

Scene 3

No longer possessed, Wai 'tu becomes the young woman she was before her capture. Though the mariner insists she is his wife, Wai 'tu denies this and begs this 'stranger' to release her. She states that her name is not Wai 'tu, but actually "Maria St. Clare". The mariner, out of obligation to his former wife, returns her from the area he originally stole her from.

Act 3

The slave revolt begins and can only be stopped by the death of innocents.

Scene 1
Realizing that the revolt is continuing without the influence of Ezili Dantor, the mariner signs aboard the first ship he sees arriving at port. They depart in haste after the mariner informs the captain of the revolt. This is kept a secret from the crew.

Scene 2
The mariner begins receiving visits from his dead children at night. He also begins hearing a voice that orders him to tell no one of what he has done. As the visits from the dead children continue, over time the mariner is filled with rage. He kills the crew out of anger, knowing that he will not be caught.

Scene 3
The mariner reveals to the narrator that he has killed everyone he has related the story to; at the urging of the voice of Ezili Dantor. He explains that this is the last time he will tell the tale, for he will kill no more. The mariner demands the narrator begin writing what he has heard by inscribing it on a pile of whale bones they are sitting near. The narrator does this with the assistance of the 3 other men listening to the story. The mariner states that once they complete their task, they are to toss the bones into the sea for the sea god to read. After this, the mariner will climb a ship mast and kill himself by jumping overboard while they witness the act.

Scene 4

Years later the narrator, as an old man himself, decides to write down the tale as we see it here. He wonders if the mariner was greeted with praise or condemnation by the gods, after he had killed so many. The narrator feels that enough time has passed that he can now reveal the haunting last words of the mariner. Before he drowned in the sea the mariner shouts out that he sees Ezili Dantor standing beside them on the dock, and points to the newly arrived narrator's wife. She calls out a name. The tale may now be told as the narrator has just drowned their children and left their bodies for his wife to discover.

THE MARINER

Eric Dean Campbell

ABOUT THE AUTHOR

Eric Dean Campbell was born and educated in Canada with a degree in film. Now retired with 20+ years of special effects for motion pictures, live events, theatre and acting, he has turned his attention to publishing the massive volume of material he has written, recorded and filmed over his lifetime.

Eric Dean Campbell

ABOUT THE ARTIST

Caspar David Friedrich was born on September 5, 1774, in Greifswald, Germany. His mother, Sophie died in 1781 when Friedrich was only seven years old.

Considered the most influential artist of his generation Freidrich changed the face of landscape paintings with his stark, provocative style. From 1794 to 1798 he studied at the world famous Copenhagen Academy. Friedrich was largely unappreciated in his era and focused on creating paintings he himself would enjoy, instead of pandering to the masses for popularity. The result was a body of startling imagery that is breathtaking to behold and appreciated by landscape lovers across time.

All images used are in the public domain.

Eric Dean Campbell

SOURCES

https://en.wikipedia.org/wiki/Caspar_David_Friedrich
https://www.britannica.com/biography/Caspar-David-Friedrich
http://www.dailyartmagazine.com/caspar-david-friedrich-works
https://commons.wikimedia.org
http://caspardavidfriedrich.net
https://www.theartstory.org/artist-friedrich-caspar-david-artworks.htm